T0198819

THE SWORD OF ILLUMIN AND OTHER STORIES

Annette Buchanan-Phillips

To order additional copies of this book, contact:
Xlibris
844-714-8691
www.Xlibris.com
Orders@Xlibris.com

ISBN: Softcover   978-1-6641-5584-8
        EBook   978-1-6641-5585-5

Print information available on the last page

Rev. date: 02/02/2021

THE SWORD OF ILLUMIN

THE SWORD OF ILLUMIN

By Annette Buchanan

Once upon a time there were two kingdoms by the sea. The kings that ruled them were friends for many years. But they grew old, and the king with the greater kingdom gave his two sons half of it to rule equally. He loved them both equally even though one was evil and one was good.

The king with the lesser kingdom had no sons, but one very beautiful and very wise daughter. The old kings had decided long ago, that one of the princes would become her husband. That son would rule the greater kingdom with her as his bride. "How shall we choose between your sons, when I have but one daughter?" The old king said to his friend. "I would certainly not wish to offend either, but the greater kingdom will belong to the son she marries." After so many years of friendship, he did not wish to cause war and anger between brothers.

"She will choose," said the father of the two princes. "We will arrange for her to visit with us for a season. Six weeks she will be the guest of each of my sons. I have divided their kingdoms across the river Illumin. There is a narrow bridge across it that will allow crossing but in one direction. That is the way of it. It has always been." The two kings looked into each other's eyes. They were silent. The father of two princes knew very well that his sons were like night and day. He had taken great pains not to favor one over the other. He had built their castles at the very farthest reach of their kingdoms. Exactly the same. Exactly at opposite corner of the land. Rivalry had always been a problem. The old king wanted to divide the kingdom ad marry one of them to the princes while he yet lived, because he knew that probably only one would survive the contest for the greatest kingdom without him. His greatest hope was to keep the peace between them.

"My daughter will travel with two guards, a cousin, and a handmaiden. She would be lonely for female company." The two old kings shook hands, saying "so be it," in unison. And so it was.

Now the princes were named Oscar and Omar. They were very similar in face. But Oscar was the elder of the two. There was one year and one month's difference in their ages. Both were equally tall and equally handsome. The castle of their father was on a bluff, overlooking the mouth of the river, Anemonie. Both sons had a large castle, equally luxurious. At the Kings request, they each agreed to be host to the Princess, her guards, her cousin and her handmaiden for the six weeks that was half a season. The Princess was named Aurora. She was accompanied by two guards, that her father had chosen. Her cousin, Aleta, and her handmaiden, who was named Laniel. They arrived at the beginning of summer. The very first day. It was very warm, and their white silken dresses floated on the gentle breeze. Aurora was not certain upon arriving at the old King's palace at which of the son's mansions that she would spend the first six weeks. So, the King, with Oscar, Omar and the Aurora's two guards present, made the toss of the coin. "Heads," called Oscar, the eldest. But the tail of the coin fell up. Omar, the younger, would be the first host. The Princess and her company went to the castle of Omar. He seemed gracious enough, his staff saw to her every need. As he had commanded, she and her company were made to feel welcome. But he was a very quiet man, somewhat distant and introspective. Omar was always pleasant and polite as befitting a Prince, but making only slight conversation at meals. He seemed preoccupied. But one night, Aurora woke and got up to look out of her window, there framed in moonlight was the silhouette of the Prince sitting in the courtyard. She felt strangely drawn to him, to know him, his thoughts, to understand his moods. From the distance, she watched him, until he felt her stare and turned, rising to look in her direction. "You are awake." He spoke not a word, from that distance she wondered if she could hear him had he shouted to her. Yet his thoughts came into her ears as clearly as if he stood beside her. His thoughts were to her very soul. "I am." She thought in return. He raised his hand, beckoning that she she should come to him in the garden. She withdrew from the window compelled to go to his call. "How can it be that he knows my soul?" She spoke out loud without realizing and her handmaiden and her cousin sat up in their beds. "Aurora!" they called out to her in one voice. "Where are you going?" The princess stopped short of the door. "Were you walking in your sleep?" Their voices prompting the guard to tap at the door. "Is there a problem, does the Princess require us?" They heard them whispering at the door. They dared not enter with her in night clothing. "Aleta, assure them that all is well. A dream woke me. Nothing more, it was only a dream." Aleta told the handmaiden, "Inform the guard." Laniel went to the door, opened but a crack and whispered. "The Princess Aurora was awakened by a dream. Nothing more. Just a dream. All is well with her." She closed the door. They could hear the message repeated at least three times in the hall. Aleta was intent to sit up until she closed her eyes. The handmaiden plumped the pillows, smoothed back the covers and stood until she climbed back into bed. "Thank you, Laniel, you may return to sleep, now. Both of you." Aurora whispered, trying not to sound annoyed. "Sweet dreams." She lay back and was covered. She closed one eye, but Aleta was content to stare until she closed the other. Aurora closed both eyes and let out a deep sigh. Aleta's bed creaked as she readjusted herself. "Shall I sit by her bed?" Laniel asked. "No, that won't be necessary. If she wakes again, we'll hear her." Aleta yawned. Laniel got back into her bed. But the Princess Aurora could see nothing but his face in the moonlight. There would be no touch of him tonight. Her eyes were closed, but the image of Omar was etched into her memory.

The rest of her stay was under the closely watchful eye of her guards. Everyone seemed especially vigilant. Daily, the fresh flowers in her room filled her senses with the intoxication of his presence. His eyes riveted hers now, in direct glances so powerful that she felt as if she were being picked up from her seat at the dining table and cradled, rocking in his arms. Without one touch, he knew her, and she knew that she was his forever. The weeks flew by. Aurora looked forward to meals, she soaked herself in the bath for hours at a time. She perfumed herself from head to toe. She plaited flowers into her hair. Should their eyes meet, she could barely turn away from his gaze. The dizziness continued. He was in her dreams, always out of reach, until the night before she was due to depart to the house of his brother. In that dream, he touched her hand. Fingers spread, then intermeshed, their bodies drew closer and at the moment of the kiss she awakened.

It was just as well; the guards were at the door, knocking. The sun was about to rise. Laniel sprang up and Aleta whispered, "Aurora." Aurora did not want to open her eyes. She wanted the night to continue. She wanted even more to stop the time, to hold the sun still in the sky and keep it from rising. Aurora did not welcome the new day, her mind was as taken as her heart. But she had the honor and the duty of the kingdom of Illumin to uphold. Stoicly, she did rise, dress and take the morning meal. He was not at the table. There would be no glimpse of Omar. She would not feel his kiss. He would not say goodbye. Aurora looked around the room. She saw every piece of furniture as if for the first time; rather than the last. She savored the colors, the smells, the smells of the house. She did not speak. Silently, she motioned to Aleta. Aleta went to thank the staff. She left Aurora's note of thanks to Omar. They departed for the castle of Omar's father. Aurora's father was there as well. He kissed her. They did have a moment alone, but Aurora barely spoke. The old King said to her softly, "Have you already lost your heart, Aurora?" She did not reply. Her eyes stung but she fought back the tears that strained to flow. "No matter," he continued. "You will keep the agreement. In six weeks you will return to me." At the midday meal, there was a great pervasive silence present. Oscar was announced, and the party did not delay their departure. It was obvious that Aurora kept the agreement to be honorable, and for no other reason.

The accommodations were actually prettier. The staff went out of their way to make them all welcome. Oscar was more communicative than his brother. He actually inquired as to her feelings. He smiled at her. She smiled, in return. But it was still Omar's voice in her ears. It was Omar in her dreams, in her thoughts, and he was the object of her desire. She looked out into Oscar's courtyard, and saw him pacing animatedly back and forth. He was discussing something with the his guards. But she remarked how much he looked like Omar. Then she acknowledged, how different that they were. She did not feel his thoughts. His words were charming but she did not believe them. She did not believe that he wanted her. She knew what he wanted. It was the power of Illumin. It was a legend that she had heard as a child. Their grand fathers had been enemies, there was a war. Aurora's grandfather was killed, and her father was crying at the river, when he saw a light in the water. He waded into the light and there at the feet of the child King was the Sword of Illumin shing as the sun. He brought out the sword from the water, and in his grief did not feel the weight of it. He drew it over his head and the light of it blinded the Warrior King of Malas. He fell from his horse upon his own sword. The two Boy Kings that were now rulers of the kingdoms of their fathers, vowed to keep the peace. And for all those years until now there seemed no reason to war ever again. Aurora's father had the secret weapon that had ended the conflict. The legend was kept within their castle walls. No one else was ever to know about the power of which she would be the next keeper. But her husband, would gain it by their marriage. Did the brothers know? She desired to know what Oscar was saying. She looked at the group again. Those were her guards. What would they be speaking about to Oscar? Who was at her guard. "Laniel, summon the guard." She went to the door but there were two of Oscar's guard outside the door. "Where are the guards of Ilumin?" she asked them. They did not reply to her. Instead they looked straight ahead. Aleta was silent during that exchange. But she looked guilty as sin. "Aleta, is something amiss that I should be informed of?" Aurora took her by the shoulders looking into her eyes. "Don't even think of lying to me, Aleta." She dropped her eyes to the floor. "It's for your own good, Aleta." Aurora looked at her with first shock and then dismay. "How can you dare to know what is best for me, Aleta?" The princess was closer to a display of anger than her cousin had ever seen. There were tears in her eyes. Tears of disillusionment. "My father ordered you to betray me. Didn't he? Say it now, or on my life I will banish you." Aleta broke down to her knees in tears. Sobbing, she admitted that her father wanted to influence her choice. She, Aleta would have the loser for her husband, and at last a kingdom of her own. "Don't hate me, Aurora. Please, don't hate me. Our fathers did arrange it all when we were born. The choice is yours to make, but Oscar has the strength to rule the greater kingdom. Both Kings know that Oscar was the stronger of the two. They want you to choose him so that the Kingdom will be strong. We will keep peace between us, maybe we will conquer new lands to rule together!" Aurora stared at her in disbelief. Aleta was a stranger to her. She stepped away from her and looked back out into the courtyard. It was deserted. "Aleta, if you are convinced that Oscar is the better man then I will share this with you. Have him. I am in love with Omar and I would rather rule with him. I am not concerned about Oscar's disapproval. I have no fear of his waging war against Illumin." That reply was apparently not what Aleta wished to hear. "You may make my apologies for the evening meal, Aleta." The Princess was sending her from the room. Aleta was about to send the message by Laniel. But Aurora insisted that she go herself. "If you see your intended face to face, be so kind as to smile. He is to be your husband. Accept it. I have chosen." Aurora turned to her handmaiden. "Turn down my bed, I will retire early." She said nothing else to either of them. Aurora took to her bed for the remainder of her stay. She pleaded that she was ill. Solemnly requesting her meals in bed, and then eating very little. She gave no explanation. But ordered Laniel, and Aleta to take their places at the table while she lay in her room. Aurora felt imprisoned, and she behaved as if she were. The weeks did elapse, however, and on the day that she was to travel, she was ready. Her guard came to escort her home. Aurora and Aleta barely spoke to each other. Everyone was extremely formal. Oscar was cold. His eyes told her that he had no intention of allowing himself to live as the elder king of the lesser kingdom. She knew that Aleta was not his choice. But the choice was hers to make. Now she understood why. There was something dark within Oscar. She did not want him to control the sword. She did not want him to rule Illumin or her. Oscar was a patient man. He knew that in order to gain the sword that he must first allow her to make her choice. He must be skillful at the proper time, then he would have both kingdoms entirely. Nothing would keep the power of All from his hands. It was his right, and if she thought that emotion would deter him from his destiny she would be surprised. Perhaps it was not a King that she wanted. Perhaps she was spoiled and willful enough to think that she was his equal. Whatever she thought really did not concern him at all. He took her hand without permission and kissed it. Looking her directly in the eyes, she recognized that he regarded her as territory not as an object of his affection. However, he did not know Aurora. He did not understand the bond that existed between Omar and her. He couldn't know. Love was not real to him. It was a vague annoyance, and interference or a means to realize his goal of ultimate power. He allowed Aurora to leave. His guard escorted her to her own border. She was furious when she entered the gate.   She was silent at the inquiry of her father. She wanted to be alone. "Three days, is all that I request of you, father. Then I shall know what is best for me and for us all." She took to her room. She dismissed both Aleta and Laniel to other quarters. Her father looked puzzled at this. But he allowed her the allotted time. Alone, the first night, she dreamed of him again. The second night, Oscar entered the dream to slay him on the bridge that she was crossing to meet him. Her own scream woke her. She feared that he would be killed if she chose him for her King. She feared he would be killed without her. That is when she decided. There was but one thing that she could do to save them both. The third day and into the night she remained in her room. But when night fell, she went into the tower behind the throne. Quietly she climbed the stairs to the place where the sword was kept. Aurora could barely raise it until she said aloud, "I must save my country, my home, my king." Then the sword began to glow. It raised itself from the floor and she did escape with it into the darkness. Uncertain as to whether she could find her way to him in the darkness, Aurora retreated back into her room. She carefully wrapped the sword in one of her bed covers and placed it gently under the bed. Every fear that she had kept her tossing and turning fretfully unable to sleep. To have the man of her dreams could mean his death. Marriage to his brother would mean the putting all power in the hands of the enemy. As dawn broke, the decision was made. The king smiled when she told him. She would marry Oscar. For the good of the kingdom she would make the sacrifice of the love of a lifetime. The preparations were made. There would be no delay. "One thing might I ask of you father. As Omar was the more gracious host and not my choice for a husband and king, may I be allowed to tell him in person. To thank him, I'd like to speak to him once again. Would that be unacceptable, father?" Aurora looked into his eyes. The King nodded. After all so great a loss might be less painful if the news were given in a delicate manner. Besides which, Aleta would be presented to him for a bride. That should make him happy. All fatherly pride aside, Aleta was actually more beautiful to behold. The power and the kingdom, rested in the marriage to Aurora. Though she was not beautiful. "As you wish, Aurora." The King agreed. The messenger was sent to the King of Abalonis. Oscar was confident. He was the victor. It was as it should be. Aleta was happy, that Omar would become her husband. He was the more handsome of the two. There would be gifts. She couldn't wait for his arrival. To claim her, would be the most natural thing. She was convinced that he would be better for having her as his queen. She began to formulate plans for the house and the grounds. She was imagining the children that they would have together and how beautiful that they would be. Aurora sat alone in her room by the window. Waiting. As the sound of his horses came into her ears, there was nothing to do but to go out to meet him. From under the bed she took out the sword of Illumin. She went down the back stairs behind the pantry, and out the door. He was about to disembark when she ran up to him carrying the wrapped sword like a baby in her arms. Omar reached out to lift her, sword in hand, up onto his horse. They rode out the gates and across the countryside finally reaching the bridge that divided their kingdoms. The bridge that would allow only one way crossing. Once inside Omar's gates Aurora took an almost normal breath. There was not a word spoken between them during their escape. It was a breathless adventure of impulse and emotion. Unreasonable to believe otherwise, Omar took his capture and the sword inside. First he kissed her. "This is for you, Omar. I fear for your safety." Aurora unwrapped the sword. She lifted J.t up between them. "May the sword of Illumin keep us safe and together." The sword began to glow. He put his hand out help her hold it up. The two of them heard at the same moment. Oscar approaches the bridge. They raised the sword up over their heads, looking into each other's eyes. "We will be free. We will be one. Yes.!" They spoke at once together. They felt the earth tremble beneath them. They began to sway with the weight of the sword that seemed to be swinging back and forth like an illuminated pendulum. Then they both saw it at the same time. The bridge was swaying and collapsed under Oscar and his guard. They were plunged to their destruction in the river below. There was sadness in their eyes as they lowered the sword.   There would be one kingdom. They would always be one, at peace forever.

THE MISFIT CHILD FROM THE PLANET ZUD

By Annette Buchanan

This is the Planet ZUD.

There once a child on the Planet ZUD. Every day he looked at his favorite book about other worlds, in other galaxies far away. In many ways, he longed to visit the Pretty Blue Planet in the Milky Way. It was called Earth. "If I could go to Earth," he said. "I'll see lots of interesting new things, and places and people." So one day he made up his mind to pack his bag and go to Earth and see how it would <u>REALLY</u> be. "I will, I will, on Earth to be." He said.

And the wings of desire swept him away to Earth. He appeared on a street and every one rushed past him. No one smiled, no one said welcome. He wondered, "Why do they walk so fast?" Where are they all going? There was noise and smoke from cars whizzing by him. And large buildings growing out of the street. They were all around him reaching into the sky. "Why does the blue stop there?" he wondered.

But looking up was a bad idea. No one noticed him and with a bump he fell down hard. "Oh My," he cried out, still holding onto his bag. But no one stopped to help. With a frown, they walked around him.

"Oh Dear!" he said, "I must be more careful here." Dusting himself off.

The sign said, "Food." He went inside. He sat right down at a table and looked around. A lady came up to him and smiled. He was overjoyed. He smiled back at her. "Okay kid, what will it be?" she asked, barely looking at him. "Food please." He asked quietly. "Hey, do you have any money?" She looked at him with a blank face, a lot like the ones outside. "Are you looking for freebies?"

"Freebies?" he said. "Oh no!"

"You'd better not be lying to me." She said.

"I am not lying. I am rich," he said telling her his name.

"Oh look here Joe, we got us a rich kid." Everyone laughed.

"So what do you want, rich kid?"

"I am very hungry." He smiled again.

"Most kids love the cheeseburger special. You want to try it?" She snarled, leaning down to him.

"Yes, thank you." He placed his bag on the seat beside him.

She walked away screaming, "Cheeseburger plate special."

"If only I knew what to say," he thought, "things would be much easier." It is very important to say the right things on Earth, he reasoned. A box up on the shelf showed little people doing funny things.

Then a very serious, loud voice interrupted. "News Bulletin!" It said.

A terrible tragedy was occurring. A war, and there were pictures of people hurt and children crying. Tears came into his eyes and rolled down his cheeks, off his chin and onto the table. The lady slammed his plate down with a glass of brown bubbling liquid.

She startled him. "Cola comes with it," she said, shoving a piece of paper beneath it. "There are the napkins, and here is the ketchup." She put down a red bottle. "I'll be back for the money, so don't try sneaking away."

She went off talking to other people. Sadly, Rich began to eat. He tasted the brown liquid, then he poured the thick red liquid on his plate like he had seen others doing. They dipped their white sticks into it and ate them and so did he. "Maybe if I do what others do, I'll fit in on Earth," he thought aloud. He had eaten half of his food when she came back. "Okay, give me the money." She turned over the paper and held out her hand. "Three fifty. Now!" She seemed cross. "Oh," he said. "No one cares about time on ZUD. We are never rushed."

"Time?" She screeched. "I knew this kid was a freeloader. Joe call the police!"

Everyone was gathered around him, yelling at once. One question after another. "Where do you live? What is your name? What is your phone number? Who are your parents?" Over and over until he began to cry. Soon men in blue clothes with sticks and tools on their belts came in. "Got another one, Joe?" They talked with very loud voices.

"Yeah, this one claimed he was rich. One of these days I'm packing in this lousey life. I mean all we ever get is a bunch of freeloaders. Get him out of here, will you? His kind is bad for business!"

"Let's go kid," they said, grabbing his arm and taking his bag from him.

    The police put him in a black and white car with red lights on top. They sat him behind a wire screen. "Okay, kid. What is your name? Where do you live? Where are your parents?" Same questions again. "I am Rich from ZUD," he said. "Wasn't I friendly enough? I tried to do what the others did with the food. Did I eat it too fast? Too slow? Why did everyone get angry with me?" Tears rolled down again. One of the police turned and looked at him through the screen. "Kid, are you on drugs?" A shrill sound came from the car as they sped away. "This kid is not responsive. Suspect drugs," he spoke into a little black box. "Better get social services in on this one."

The child from ZUD looked out the window as he was whisked down street after street. Blank faces stopped to stare, and he wondered why he ever wanted to come to Earth. The Pretty Blue Planet in the sky was very ugly from the ground. The car stopped. This building looked cold and mean. The people inside stared at him. He felt truly afraid.

"Hello young man," a lady smiled at him. "Can we talk for a moment?" she took him by the hand and took his bag in the other. She lead him into a white room. There was a small table and chair. "Please sit down, I won't hurt you. I'm here to help you," she smiled again.

Sadly, he sat down.

"I guess you were a little too frightened to tell the nice policemen your name and address. But you can tell me okay?" He looked at her with big brown eyes, that were full of tears. "Now, now don't cry," she said, dabbing tissue up to the overflow. "I'm from the Child Welfare Department. I promise you that all I want to do is to contact your family. They will come here and take you home. Are you lost? Is that what happened? How about some ice cream?" She looked into his eyes. He looked at her sadly, still not speaking.

"I know what we can do that will be fun! I'll give you paper and crayons and you can write your name and address for me." Trying to look pleasant. She put a piece of paper and crayons before him. Then took his hand and guided him to make a mark. She left the room. Rich was alone but she was watching him through a secret window. He drew on the paper. When he was finished, he took five seeds from his pocket and ate them. "I will to be, returned to thee, on ZUD I am." And he was gone. "He disappeared!" The woman shrieked. She ran into the room to see what he had written on his paper.

This is what she saw.

Patti Pigs Out!

PATTI PIGS OUT!

By Annette Buchanan

The sweet smell of something in the kitchen woke Patti up. Her nose wriggled, she sniffed three times and her eyes opened wide. "Oh my," she said, rubbing he eyes. Patti rolled out of bed, jumped into her fuzzy bunny slippers. She ran for the kitchen. "Hi Patti," aproned mother gave her head a big kiss. "You're awake early, want some breakfast?"

Patti smiled a wide, one tooth missing smile. She yawned, she stretched, "I'm hungry." Patti peeked around her mother. She was looking for that good smell. "Go wash up for breakfast, Patti." Mother turned her around by the shoulders and pointed her toward the bathroom. Off she padded in her big fuzzy bunny shoes. She washed fast. Then back to the kitchen.

    Mother pulled out her chair, and Patti sat down to the table. She was waiting for a taste of that delightful smell. Mother sat a bowl of cereal in front of her. A glass of juice and a piece of sausage. She looked at Patti, "all right honey, eat your breakfast." A big frown came out on Patti's face. None of this food was the right smell. She sniffed it all. "Patti! What are you doing?" Mother scolded. "That's rude. Mind your manners young lady!"

Patti picked up the spoon reluctantly. She began to eat slowly. She blew her bubbles in her juice through the straw she always got. She bit her sausage and tapped out sounds on her plate. She splashed milk in her cereal bowl. Milk landing on the table always got a raised eyebrow from mother. "I thought you said you were hungry, Patti. You're playing in your food. Is there a problem?" Patti displayed her best pout. She put her elbows on the table. She twisted her legs around the chair. "This is all the wrong stuff!" she pushed the bowl away and folded her arms.

"If you are finished, you may leave the table." Mother began washing the dishes. Patti sat defiant. Not eating. Not moving. When the other dishes were finished mother took away the bowl. She washed it. Patti sat still hungry, but determined. Next, the piece of sausage went. The plate was washed and stacked. Patti was still defiant. Only the juice was left. They looked at each other. Mother paused to give her one last chance. But Patti had a will of steel. She folded her arms and legs. Away went the juice. Poured out into the sink. And down the drain.

Mother washed the glass, wiped off the table wetly. Too wet for Patti's elbows. Mother did not say a word. She just walked away to choose Patti's clothes for the day. "Come put on clean things, Patti." Mother was strained. Patti could tell that voice. "Now!" She almost shouted. Patti did not want to push too close to the punish line. She abandoned the chair, but just to prove she had temper too, she pushed her chair up to the table hard. Mother put her hands on her hips and tapped her foot. Patti ran past her and slammed her door. Mother heaved a deep sigh and went straight for a relaxing bath.

She didn't hear Patti tiptoe down the hall. She went to the kitchen. She looked around. There on top of the counter was a glass plate with a pretty cover. Patti pulled up a chair. She climbed up on it. She took off the cover. There it was! A pie!!! Boy did it smell good. Patti stuck in a spoon. She ate. And she ate. She ate so much, that she didn't hear mother come out of the bathroom. She ate so long that mother found her room empty when she came to check on her. "Patti, where are you?" Mother called out.

It did not take long to find out. Patti jumped from the chair and ran back to her room. Pie was still on her face. But not much was on her mother's pie stand. The day dragged on and not a word was said about the pie. Company came for dinner. Father came home from his trip. Everyone had hugs and kisses for Patti. They all sat down to eat. There were six with Patti. She kept staring at the covered pie stand. She knew there was no pie.

She looked sadder and sadder. Everyone kept saying what a good girl she was. "You have such a well mannered child." One lady commented. "Yes, we are very proud of Patti." Her father smiled. "Well, how about dessert everyone? I hope it tastes good. It's Patti's favorite." As her mother rose from the table to get the pie, Patti began to cry loudly. "I'm sorry!" She cried out. "What's the problem Patti?" Father reached out to her. "Tell me, now what could be worth all these big tears?" He said wiping them with large fingers. "Ahhh! Ahhh! I pigged out the pie!" Patti barely got it out. "I was bad. I ate it when Mom took her bath."

    Everyone started to laugh. Patti wiped her eyes. Mother sat down the most beautiful Apple Pie Patti had ever seen? Mother smiled and gave her a big hug. "I think you learned a lesson Patti, sit down and have some pie. Well, dear? Patti sat down. And everyone loved the pie. And father hugged mother because she baked two pies. "Patti, father is proud of you for admitting your mistake, and apologizing for it. Next time you'll ask first. Okay?" Patti nodded, and mother hugged her. "We love you." They kissed her. Everybody laughed.

BOBBY'S
MAGIC
BRUSH

BOBBY'S MAGIC BRUSH

By Annette Buchanan

Happy Birthday Bobby! Everyone sang. Bobby smiled. On the birthday cake, candle flame danced. "Make a wish, son. Now blow out the candles," said father. Mother held up her camera to take the picture. Bobby made his wish. He took in a big breath, and blew out all six candles at once. "What did you wish?" His brother wanted to know. "It's a secret, right?" Little Sara chimed in. Bobby blinked. The flash from his mother's camera made everything one big red spot.

But he ripped the paper from the first gift someone put into his hands. His eyes focused on a beautiful set of Artist's Paints, and brushes made of real sable hairs. They were beautiful with golden tips at the ends of white stems. "It's just what I wanted! It's Magic!" Bobby exclaimed. Mother kissed him, and took another picture to capture the wish come true. All of the other presents were wonderful too. But Bobby couldn't take his eyes off the Magic Art Set. He just couldn't wait to paint his imagination. That night he went to sleep smiling, and holding his Magic Brush.

He dreamed of a beautiful sky, and he thought it would make a beautiful painting. But then he changed his mind and painted clouds that were dark, and thunder and lightning began to appear. The sound of that rumbling thunder, and the crackle of that lightning woke him up. "It really is magic! I can have all that I wish for, by painting it! Wow! I must paint only good things." Bobby lay back down, for a while. It rained all morning. There was no school, and Bobby went back to his room after breakfast. His paint cup full of water, he sat down at his desk.

He painted the beautiful sunny sky that he first saw in his dream. He painted white fluffy clouds floating on the most beautiful blue sky. He painted a bright yellow sun and flowers. He painted himself smiling. So absorbed was he in his painting that he didn't notice the time going by. When he had finally finished painting, everyone had already eaten lunch. "isn't it a beautiful spring day?" Mother said looking up from her reading. Bobby ran to the window and looked out the sun was shining brightly. He saw that sun and could barely believe his eyes.

"It's true!" he exclaimed. "It is magic." Mother chuckled. "Bobby, everyone else has eaten and are gone out to play. Why don't you eat your sandwich now, and you can go out for some fresh air." Nothing could convince Bobby that his paint brush wasn't magic now. He ate his lunch in a hurry and ran out to ride his bike. But not before tucking his magic brush in his back pocket. He his brother Reg, and Sara played until dinner time. They were having so much fun that Bobby forgot all about the Magic Brush. But after dinner, and his bath, he looked over at his desk before getting into bed, but no brush was there. Where is it? He thought to himself. He became frantic.

Searching everywhere, on the desk, on the floor, under his bed, but it was not there. He searched the kitchen. He searched the living room. He searched the dirty clothes hamper, and under the bathroom rug. But it was not there. I've lost my Magic Brush. Now I can't paint my wishes to be true! Tears were in his eyes. Bobby was turning over the pillows on the couch. Father stopped him when one of them hit the floor. "Bobby! What do you think that you are doing, young man?" Father said. "Well?" "I can't find my Magic Brush!" Bobby answered, still searching. "Just a minute son," father said calmly. "Now, what is this that you're telling me? What Magic Brush? And just what makes you think that you ever had a Magic Brush, Bobby?"

Father had that waiting for a good explanation look on his face. He seemed somehow taller than usual. Bobby took a deep breath. This story had to be told just right for father to believe it. "Yesterday when I blew out my candles and made a wish for my birthday I got the Art Set that I wished for and ever since then I can make wishes come true with my Magic Brush." He exhaled. Father shook his head. He scratched his beard. "Two things," he said slowly sitting down to Bobby's level. "First, I'm glad you liked the gift your mother and I gave you, but I assure you it's only magic if you believe it is. The real magic is that wonderful imagination of yours, son." Father smiled at him.

His eyes twinkled. "Second, it's dark out now, look for it tomorrow when it's light. Off to bed with you." He gave Bobby a hug. He knew Bobby was not convinced. "I know that the Magic is you son, not the paint brush. Any old brush would be the same in your hands. Try believing in yourself. You'll see." Bobby went up to his room. He thought to himself, but nothing was magic before. He looked at his painting. He looked at the other brushes. He picked them up. It just didn't feel the same. The magic was gone. Bobby wished he could find his Magic Brush. He lay down to go to sleep. But he tossed and turned. Maybe he would find it.

He slept. He dreamed of fun, and playing with Sara, and her little puppy. He dreamed that Boxy had his Magic Brush and ran off with it when he and Sara were riding. But where did the puppy hide that brush? Bobby woke up wondering. Could it be true? Did Boxy hide that Magic Brush? Bobby could hardly wait till Sara and her puppy came out to play. He heard her mother tell her not to ride too near to the street. He ran outside. They nearly bumped into each other. "Isn't this the paint brush you got for your birthday, Bobby?" Sara barely could stay on her feet because Bobby hugged her so hard. "It's true! Father was right. The magic is in me." Sara looked puzzled. "Boys are so weird!" Sara jumped on her bike and rode off smiling, with Boxy beside her.

Jumping happily. Now, Bobby knew. He could never lose the Magic. He believed.

The End.

By Annette Buchanan 3/22/94@11a

YES I CAN!! BOOKS

A FROG NAMED PRINCE

By Annette Buchanan

A FROG NAMED PRINCE

By ME:
Annette Buchanan

A FROG NAMED PRINCE

One day in a kingdom not so far away, a little Princess sat looking out of her window. "Oh –what a bright and sunny day," she thought aloud, "I will go and ask my mother, the Queen, if I might go out and play beyond the palace walls." The little Princess jumped from her window seat and ran to find her parents. She ran from room to room calling out for her mother and father. When she finally found them, they were busy at work on the kingdoms finances. "I beg the King's per- mission to go out to play beyond the palace walls in the sun," she said politely. Her father the King looked over the rim of his glasses at her, frowning in decision making fashion. "Our daughter the Princess wishes to play beyond the palace walls today Queen Mother, what say you to this request?" Her mother, the Queen looked first at her shoes, then assessed her apparel. "Those shoes, are the finest that the Princess has to wear," she said looking back to her paperwork.   "However, if she should be seen by any visiting dignitaries she will make a royal first impression. Therefore, King, if it is well with thee, it is well with me." The little Princess was nearly jumping by now with the anticipation of approval; after all she was the King's little darling. This she was quite confident of, everybody said so. The pause was so long though, she thought if there was a remote possibility of refusal, now was the time to give her adoring look and her most charming, persuasive smile. "Well, Princess, if you promise not to stray into the forest or the town, I will allow it."

"Oh, most wonderful King and father, I promise. I solemly swear," pleaded the little Princess. Many townsgirls were thinking of marriage at this age she thought, being ripe old and all of six- teen. Being a Princess has certain disadvantages. Permission to breathe, being one of them. Notwithstanding, no other kingdoms existed for miles and finding a suitable suitor would be near to improbable at best. Yet one never knows but that some handsome stable boy might risk his future for the privilege of teaching her, the Princess to kiss.

"Very well Princess, and do not stray," admonished the King. Delighted, the Princess uttered her thank you's on the way out the door.

At last, the world outside these walls would bask in her glory, how long the world has waited to know and love her; and now the appointed time has arrived. She stopped for a few seconds before the hall mirror to take stock of her appearance. It would not do for a Princess to be seen with her hair out of place, or crumbs on her face, or heaven forbid, dusty shoes. When she was assured that she looked quite perfect, she opened the door to the world. The bright light of the summer's day made her squint at first, but then she was reminded that squinting was a determined cause of early wrinkles in delicate skin like hers, so said the Queen. Before her stretched the walkway and the little bridge that crossed the moat. Everyday it was let down in the morning after breakfast, and let up in the evening after dinner. It was, today an open invitation to adventure. The Princess sat down on the bench beneath the willow across the road. The birds chirped, the squirrels played, the bees stopped to do business with flowers, but not one person passed by. Determined to have her dreams become reality, she wandered down the hill, away from the palace, to the open road.

The road went to town, she was certain of that, but which way was which, she was not quite sure. There is no danger, of becoming lost, after all everyone in the kingdom knew her. Besides that, she would not go far because her little white pumps would not allow it. The path she chose led her into a thicket. The road itself began to narrow and then disappear. The trees became more thickly bunched together, and the sunlight seemed to only trickle through. "OOO!" The hoot of the owl frightened her and she tripped over roots grown up over the forest floor, covered with last autumn's leaves. Perhaps she hit her head upon a stone, or something, because when she opened her eyes again, there was just the barest light to be seen. "Oh no, my dress, my shoes, my hair," she said brushing bits of leaf and moss and dust from herself. "I must get back to the palace, there is not one mirror here and if anyone should see me they won't even recognise me with this dirt all over me. I know that dinner will be soon and I must have my bath. I will go home to the palace this very minute," she cried decidedly. Looking around her, there was not one familiar tree, nor anything that even remotely favored the path she had travelled to get to this awful place. The Princess started to run, not certain that she was going in the right direction. Hopelessly lost, she sat down on fallen log and began to sob bitterly aloud. "I want my mother, the Queen, and my father, the King and my wonderful home and my beautiful bed and my tub and my maid and my combs and my mirror. Why did I ever leave the palace?" She screamed louder and louder.

"Help me please someone, anyone, I'm the Princess; and I demand to be found this instant. But the only reply that came back was the songs of the nightfall, made by crickets and owls until... "Excuse me, some of us hunt at night and you are disturbing the catch with that infernal howling. You're scaring away the food, get it big mouth?" The Princess, startled mid howl, shut up and looked about to see where that welcome, albeit rude voice was coming from. Dark ness not withstanding, she inquired in a much more composed Princess tone, "To whom am I speaking, if I may be so bold?" She was still looking around, not seeing a soul.

"Someone who will be quite hungry this evening if you don't shut up!, apparently."

"I demand that you identify yourself immediately, and reveal your face to the Princess Elenna this instant or face the charge of insubordination." She was most like her father, the King, when insulted or perturbed you know. It was for certain that not even this extremely contemptuous voice in the darkness could tell that she was more frightened than she ever dreamed imaginable.

"My name, if it's any of your business, is Prince," the voice called back obviously unimpressed by her demands. "Quite frankly, you are no Princess of mine and you are an intruder in my kingdom, and upsetting my endeavors. If anyone should be insulted, it is I. If any demanding gets done around here, I'll be doing it. So kindly get out of my kingdom right now, trespasser! Or you will be thrown out, posthaste." With that the Princess sank to the ground howling louder than ever.

"I can't," she cried, "I'm lost, and frightened and hungry. If I leave this spot I may fall prey to wolves, or bears and even pirates or Princess snatchers," she lamented pitifully yet not undecidedly charming; hoping to appeal to any latent compassion that might be laying dormant in this brutish but desperately needed and possibly rescuing person. "I beg your pardon, sir I had no way of discerning in the darkness, that you were of royal personage like myself. I pray you please forgive me," she said sweetly. Who knows but she may have found her dreams here, lost in the forest, in the dark. She desperately wished she had been more presentable and less presumptuous. Hopefully, Prince whoever, would take her to his palace and his family would embrace her. They might even marry and join their kingdoms. Her fantasy was interrupted by a croak and a rustle of leaves.

"You are forgiven," he said curtly. The voice seemed to be a little farther away. More leaves rustled. The Princess panicked, realizing he may just leave her there just as he had found her.

"Kind sir, I know that I am forward to ask, but would you be so kind as to take me to your palace for the night. It is surely past dinner and I am tired and dirty from my fall. It is not probably your custom to take in strangers, even if they are Princesses no doubt. But I know that if you will take me home by morning light my father will certainly reward you." She desperately hoped that her plea was not mistaken for a beg, but she was not altogether sure it should matter when lost in the forest in the dark. If begging would be more greatly appreciated it could probably be accomplished just this once under these extenuating circumstances. At worst it would be a matter for interpretation. It is most definately difficult to maintain a royal demeanor when lost and dirty in the forest at night.

"Hmmm...," he made a sound of disgusted imposition.

"I promise," she said struggling to acquiece, "I will be no trouble at all. Not even to your servants, I will even make my own bed down; and I require no assistance at all with my bath once the tub is drawn. Really, and in the morning light, I will thank all and you or your servants may show me home. If you please, sir."

"We'll see how long you keep those vows," he mumbled unbelieving. "All right follow me." She certainly did not wish to antagonize him by mentioning the fact that she still couldn't see him, so when she saw a movement of leaves a little way ahead of her, she followed it. Finally, there came in the midst of the trees, a clearing. The moon shimmered upon the glassy looking surface of what appeared to be a pond. There were seven stones that crossed it and lily pads in bloom floated serenely in adornment. A cave or a hollow of some kind was all that she saw on the other side.

"Prince," she called out, "is it much further?" She called out again to him, but no reply came back. Testing the first stone with her foot to be certain it would support her, she stepped onto it and in that manner, carefully made her way to the shelter in sight.   Once inside, she looked about as far as moonlight would allow. A few leaves at the mouth of the hollow, she gathered together to make her bed and her white petticoat she spread down to lay on. Weariness overtook her quickly, crying quietly Princess Elenna drifted to sleep.

The early sun flooded the hollow with so much brightness that her eyes blinked several times to adjust to the light of day. For a few second confusion took hold of her and no signs of her familiar surroundings gave her to panic.   Springing to her knees the Princess rubbed her eyes for a better look. The memories of yesterday came back to her, and so did the tears. She wailed, she beat the ground with her fists, all to no avail. She wished as hard as she was able for angels to appear and carry her home. How long she lamented is not known but after a time the tears stopped and the loud realization of hunger set in. Just inside the hollow, near where her head had been, she suddenly noticed several pieces of fruit. There were apples and pears, peaches and plums. Along side of which she saw what looked like nuts. The kind her maids cracked for her at special times. Her parents, the King and Queen, set them out for and she would linger the kitchen following the cooks in their preparations. They must all be crying for her now, as much as she was crying for them. Sadly, Elenna picked up some fruit and washed them in the pond. The birds sang, the lily pads danced with the ripples she created. There by the water, she became aware the exquisite beauty and peace of her surroundings here. Even the stillness possessed immense activity, the busy butterflies paused but for a second to allow her just enough time to admire their colors. On the other side of the pond two squirrels played together, chasing each other from branch to low slung branch of a tall tree. She took a bite of the apple as she watched them, and its sweet juiciness touched her soul by way of her tongue.   "Umm, I've never had such a delicious apple in all of my kingdom," she heard herself speaking aloud to no one apparent. The squirrels paused at the sound of her voice looking in her direction as if annoyed at her interruption. "Excuse me," she said to them when she noticed that they were now aware of her. The apple experience was over all too quickly because she decided to eat another fruit to see if it could possibly be as rare and wonderful. Once satiated, she looked into the mirrored surface of the still again pond, and decided she looked terrible. Bending over, the Princess cupped her hands to gather enough water to wash her face but it kept falling through her fingers. It is certainly impossible to accomplish a bath in this fashion, she realized after a few unsuccessful attempts. Therefore perhaps it might be better to start from the other end, she deduced all this in quite princessly fashion of course. So she sat down flat on the ground and moved herself to venture in a toe or two, then a foot. Surprisingly the water was a very tepid not quite war but certainly not cold. She dipped both feet up to her slender ankles, then she risked her calves, but fearing that she might fall in, she stopped at the knees. That's when she realized that it was no deeper than a pool to swim in near the palace, and jumped in. There was only one problem with bathing in one's clothes, and that was that there was no armoire full of choices of beautiful things to wear afterward. "Oh well," she thought, "I'll just enjoy this fun now and worry about all those other things later." Eventually, she had to get out of the water, though and with no maid to help her she put on the dry petticoat. Now I'll have no bed if I'm not home soon, she reasoned. "Hmmm, what would be the proper thing to do now to correct this situation?" She mused for a moment then reflected upon days in the yard with the laundress hanging the clothes outside the palace kitchen. "I know, I will hang these wet things in the sun and they will be fresh as my things when the laundress did them." Elenna, stepped out onto the stones that brought her across the pond to hang her wet things on the low branches of the squirrel's tree. Looking around herself in all directions she discovered the apple trees, and the others that had provided her breakfast. "How did those fruit get together all the way over there?" She wondered aloud. "Prince must have done it. Feeling someone's eyes upon her, she turned around abruptly, hoping that he was there. Sadly, there was not a soul in sight except a frog sitting atop one of the lily pads. "Oh," she said half to the frog, half to herself disappointedly. "I thought that you were the Prince who found me in the woods last night and brought me breakfast this morning. I hoped that he was come to take me home or to his kingdom. Well, actually if you had been him I would have been most embarrassed to receive his highness in a petticoat. My clothes, you see are drying there." She pointed to where they hung on the branches. The frog said not a word but hopped from the lily pad into the water and swam about for a bit. "By the time the Prince returns or I am found by the King's soldiers I will most certainly be considered mad: to think, I'm talking to frogs and squirrels and butterflies. Please someone, come soon," suddenly the tears came swelling up in her eyes again. Across the pond, stone by stone she fought them until finally on the other side she sat down heavily sobbing. "Ribbit, ribbit," croaked the frog beside her. She opened her eyes, wiping her hands across her face. The greenish brown frog peered at her. "I wish you were the Prince," she moaned, "but you're just a frog. You can't help me at all." There was a definite pout on her lips.   The frog just sat there looking at her saying nothing. But when she tried to touch it, it hopped away across the pond from lily pad to lily pad and out of sight back into the forest. "I didn't mean it," she cried out after it, "please come back at least a frog is better than no one at all." It did not come back. "I certainly did not mean to be insulting, actually the frog could have tried a little harder to understand my circumstances not to mention my obvious disappointment." The Princess began to cry afresh, "if the frog ever forgives me, if it ever comes back to play in this part of the forest; I will be more kind. I will be more respectful of its feelings, after all frogs must certainly have delicate sensibilities. Yes, I will be much, much more considerate of frogs in the future. Frogs do have value too, don't they? " Wearily, she lay down to rest upon her bed of leaves. More fruit was left for her in the hollow. Mentally listing the value and purposes for frogs and squirrels and bees and butterflies she closed her eyes. It was mid afternoon and the clothes were dry. Princess Elenna was dressed and ready for the Prince to come and lead her out of the forest. She would have gone off alone but fear kept her from trying. She had images of being even lost from the hollow and the pond and what if the Prince should come and she was not here. This was where he had led her. Perhaps the journey was too far and he had gone to bring her back help of some kind. She waited. And waited. She ate more fruit, and waited, but he did not come. The sun went down, and more tears came up. The full bright moon lit up the clearing and cast eery shadows around. The Princess lay atop her soft bed of leaves listening to the songs of the crickets. Night sounds in the forest made by owls are very frightening to a lonely young lady when lost. So she lay still inside the hollow. Then a most familiar, welcome voice said, "how do you like my kingdom?" At first uncertain that she actually had heard what she thought she heard she sat up abruptly. "Is this an apparition of voice that comes to my ears, or is it really you, Prince?"

"It is I. Now tell me, how do you like my kingdom?" he insisted. Not wishing to offend, but slightly disillusioned the Princess was hesitant to answer. What she wanted to say was how uncomfortable her bed was, how dark her accommodations, and how limited her choice of food and clothing; but not wishing to repeat the frog incident, she graciously replied, "I am most grateful for all of your kindnesses sir. The breakfast was exceptionally tasty, and I made friends of squirrels and a frog," she lied. "Have you come to take me home?" By now she was at the mouth of the hollow looking anxiously in all directions. To her dismay, she saw no one, "Prince?" There was a small splash in the pond and the moonlight made the ripples look like jeweled ribbons in the darkness. "Froggie? the name came about naturally, thoughtlessly. "Someone, anyone?" Dejected, she returned to her bed of leaves. "Maybe, tomorrow he'll come again." She thought it, she said it, she sang herself to sleep, "maybe tomorrow, he'll come to me. Tomorrow, he'll set me free, tomorrow."

The morning came, but he did not. She had eaten the last of yesterday's fruit, so the first thing that was required for this day must surely be more of it. Stepping lightly now confident in the stones beneath her she proceeded to find her meals. Hoping for low branches, but knowing that she was capable of a short climb, she gathered more fruit than she could possibly want for one day. Placing them in her skirts she carried across one pile and then another. When she had finished, the Princess applauded her own accomplishment. "Look what I have done for myself," she said proudly. "I have been lost, I have found shelter, I have made me a bed, I have gotten me food, I have made me new friends, I have made the best of this terrible situation and survived. I'm truly a Princess, and truly wonderful." Then she went to the pond to wash herself. In the pond her own reflection looked somehow different to her. It was probably that she had to admit that she had had help. "Well," she said, replying to her own thoughts, "the Prince did help when he led me to this place, and he did show me there was food available when he left my first breakfast. The stones helped when they made the bridge across the pond and the hollow helped by being there to sleep in and the trees helped by bearing the fruit that was my food. The squirrels helped to ease my lonliness, the sun and the moon lit the day and the night; but the frog, the frog did nothing." She washed and returned to her hollow. Once fully dressed, she sat down to eat. Her routine was now established. "Ribbit, Ribbit, Ribbit," interrupted the frog. Princess Elenna paused midbite, not able to reply with a full mouth, she completed her chewing. "You came back," she smiled broadly," first let me apologize for having implied on yesterday that your company and friendship were not of the highest value to me." She took another bite. "Polite conversation is not everything, you know. Besides that, pleasant company is most always appreciated; especially in times of trouble and lonliness. Believe me, I just want you to stay, even if you don't say a word besides "ribbit." She imitated laughing. "See, I can speak frog language if I try. Ribbit, ribbit, ribbit. See?" She continued to munch on the pears, and apples. The frog hopped across the pond on the stones and back again to the Princess. "Oh," she sprang to her feet quickly, "you want to play?" The frog hopped across the stones and back in the same fashion. "Oh, now I get it. You want me to follow you!" The frog hopped to the other side and waited. It occurred to the Princess that she could very possibly play too far from her new home like she did from her old home. However, she was now confident that she could survive anywhere, under any circumstances. Afterall, if anyone knew the forest the frog should, he lived there. Without another thought, the Princess followed him. They hopped through the forest, they played and before long they came to the road. There, across the road and up the hill the Princess saw her home, her beloved palace. "Froggie, you're wonderful!" She stooped and picking him up in her hands she kissed him. "If only you were an enchanted Prince who would marry me and be my hero forever. But I love you just as you are, and I want you to come and stay with me in the palace. You are my hero, I love you." With tears in her eyes she kissed him again. "You love me even though I'm a frog and will always be a frog?" He said. She dropped him, amazed that he spoke. "You are the Prince?" She shrieked, "you know that I thought you were a man. I thought that you had a kingdom. I thought..."

"You were right about some things and wrong about others. My name is Prince, that is what you asked me wasn't it? I took you to my home and kingdom like you asked me to, didn't I? I shared my home and hospitality with you and then you insulted me because I was a frog. So now, here you are. Go home and be a snotty Princess. I'm certain that a frog will be easy to forget. I guess you are a liar too, saying you love me and taking it back when I don't live up to your fantasy. Now that you know me for my true self, am I less of a Prince and more of a frog?" His arrogance was at least shy of total. The Princess Elenna was taken back his lack of tact, but she knew he was right about her. There was silence, but truth was loudly demanding her answer to his charges. "I...... she stammered, "apologized for the insult, and if I lied it was out of fear of lonliness and I meant everything I told you. Now that I know that you can talk we'll have even more fun together and share lots of secrets and be the best of friends."

"If you really mean it, then kiss me again knowing full well that I am a frog and will be a frog forever, and I will believe you." Prince said smugly. The Princess knew that if she did not kiss him that she would be three times the liar, but somehow she had to admit that she had believed in fairy stories of frogs turning into Princes when kissed by a true Princess. Therefore she swallowed hard and picked up Prince, closed her eyes and kissed him. To her amazement he became the most beautiful Prince she had ever seen or imagined. "I thought you said that you would be a frog forever," she grinned gleefully. "You're beautiful."

"I lied.   I was looking for someone who would love me for myself. "He kissed her back. "So, let's go meet the folks."

--- The End ---

Printed in the United States
By Bookmasters